PAPERBOY IV

L .O.E.P.'S WORST NIGHTMARE

By

Omari Jeremiah

Illustrations by Bernie Rollins

MORTON BOOKS, Inc.

FIRST MORTON BOOKS EDITION
Copyright 2007, Omari Jeremiah

Morton ISBN:978-1-929188-15-4
Cover design by Bernie Rollins
www.robmorton.com

Printed in the United States of America

This book is dedicated to:

My sister, Aquisha Jeremiah,

My mother and father,

My brother, Osei,

My Aunt Pat and Uncle Darryl,

My cousin, DJ,

My cousin, Chris, and his mother, Julia

My Grand-mother, and Fabian

My publicist, Ms. Holland,

My loving niece, Skyla Jeremiah,

Mr. Robert Hannibal, Principal of Ms. 145, and

Ms. Deborah Christian, one of my favorite teachers.

Thanks for your prayers and support.

Contents

Undefeatable enemies appear

A hero's dark side is revealed ……

And Shorty gets his revenge….

Soon after his escape from P.S. 244, Paperboy returns to school to find a mysterious figure lurking there; Shadow Paperboy. Shadow Paperboy's identity is as mysterious as his sudden appearance. But Shadow Paperboy is after something and he won't stop until he gets it.

Can Paperboy find out who Shadow Paperboy is? Or will he ever know the truth behind this powerful new individual?

Chapter 1

New Heroes

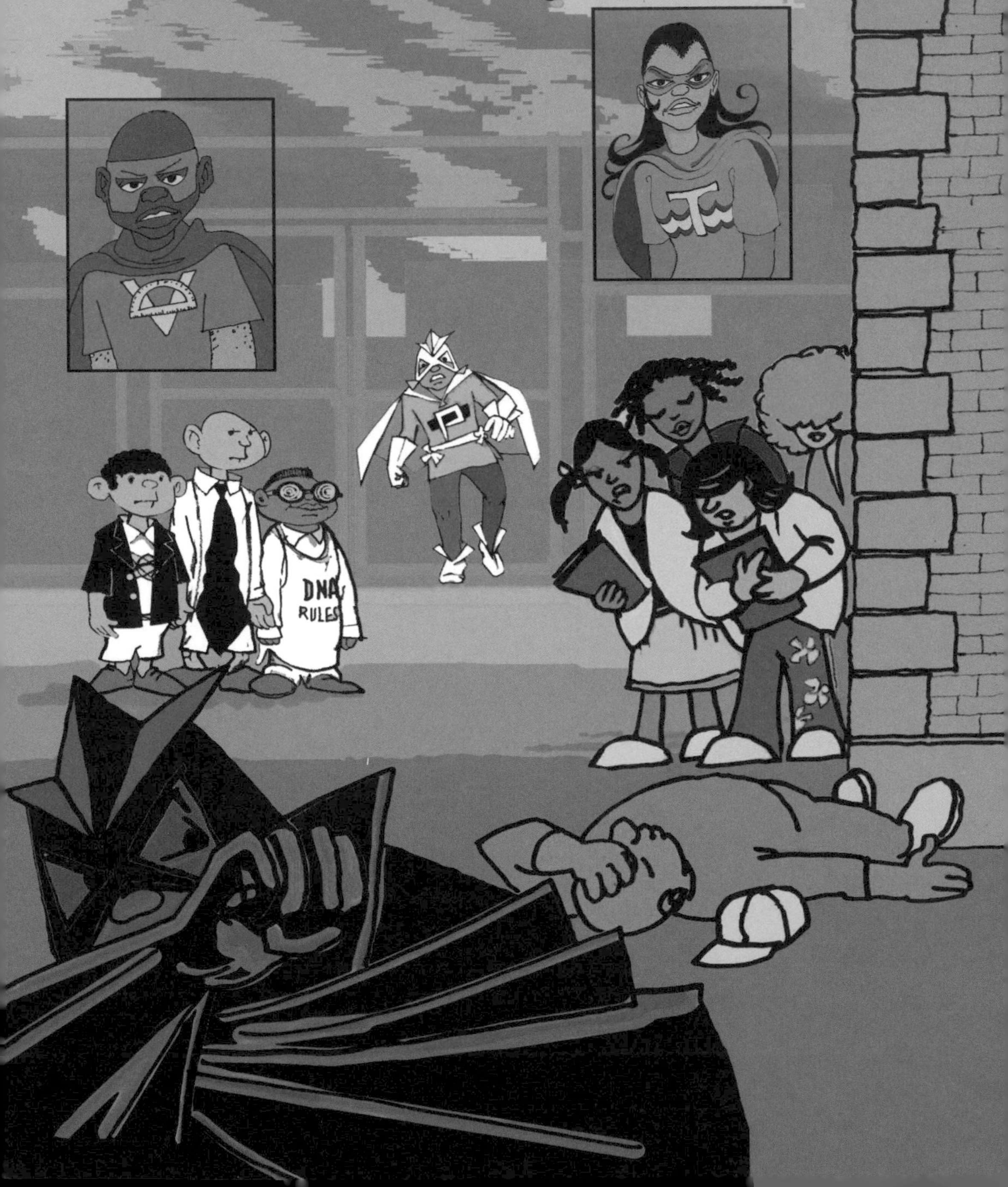

ONE

"Michael! Get ready for School!"

"Okay, mom."

"Breakfast is on the table!"

"Okay, mom."

"I'm going to work now! Have a good day!"

"Bye, mom."

Michael got up from his bed. It had been more than three days since they escaped P.S. 244. Michael sighed. In such a short time his life had changed so much. Mr. Raptor turned out to be his father, he had a brother named Scott who also fought LOEP (League of Evil People) and he learned that LOEP controlled Scott's school, P.S. 244. Michael sighed again. He knew that without his friends, he would have been overwhelmed by this. He was happy he had people to help him.

With that thought in mind, Michael got up and stretched. He took a shower, got dressed, went downstairs, ate breakfast and changed into his Paperboy costume. Paperboy rode his Papermobile to P.S. 266. Once there, he chained the Papermobile to the gate and put a padlock on it. Paperboy then raced into P.S. 266.

Once inside he dashed into the janitor's closet and changed.

Michael walked out of the janitor's closet and to his classroom. Inside the classroom, Michael noticed Miss Rex writing on the chalkboard. He also noticed that the chalkboard was brimming with words. Big words! Words Michael had never seen or even knew existed. Michael sat in his seat and turned around. In back of him sat Nina. The two greeted each other. Michael then turned around to face Miss Rex.

"You will have a test on each word on this board in two days," Miss Rex announced.

The class groaned. Michael silently wrote down the words on a sheet of paper. After that, Miss Rex went over the definitions of all the big words. Michael absorbed Miss Rex's words like a sponge.

Behind him, Nina thought of reasons why giving a test on such big words should be a crime.

Half an hour later, the bell rang for recess. Michael walked out of class and into the janitor's closet to change. Minutes later, Paperboy walked out of the janitor's closet and out to the playground.

Outside, Paperboy saw Nina talking to her friends. He also saw a nerd being pushed around by a bully. But before Paperboy could reach the bully, a dark figure appeared. Paperboy gasped. The dark figure looked almost like him. But instead of having white paper airplanes, PBB's, paper lasers and paper claws, they were all black. The figure had a black evil looking mask. Paperboy watched as the black figure attacked the bully mercilessly with his black paper airplanes. The bully fell to the ground. The dark figure took out a black paper laser and fired it. The little black paper balls hit the bully and he cried out in pain. The dark figure ran to the gate and climbed to the other side. Then as mysteriously as he came, the dark figure left.

Paperboy stood in shock for one minute. Most of the students in the playground saw the incident. They glanced at Paperboy. Unfortunately, the gossiping girls had seen the incident also. Five minutes later a rumor started to spread about the incident. Paperboy overheard two nerds talking about the rumor.

"They say that the dark figure who attacked the bully was Shadow Paperboy. The other nerd explained, "Shadow Paperboy is Paperboy's dark side. It will attack anyone it chooses to." The nerds then walked away.

Paperboy sighed in disbelief. Who was Shadow Paperboy? Why did Shadow Paperboy attack that bully? And how did he know Paperboy's weapons and how to use them? Suddenly the bell rang. With these questions in mind, Paperboy went back into P.S. 266.

Later that day, Michael, James, Nina and Scott walked to Michael's house. Michael opened the door. They went up to Michael's room.

"I'm going to start my homework," Michael announced.

"Me too," Scott agreed.

Michael and Scott sat on Michael's bed and started their homework, leaving James and Nina standing in the middle of the room. They looked at each other, then James spoke.

"Actually, we have something to show you," James said, pointing to Nina.

They both went downstairs. Scott and Michael looked at each other, puzzled. Suddenly, James and Nina came back upstairs in costumes. James wore a cape. He also had on roller skates and protractors were on his hands. James' mask was green as was the rest of his costume. Michael noticed that protractors also hung from James' roller skates.

Nina's costume was blue. It consisted of a blue mask and a cape. She had a water pen in each hand and some in her pockets. She turned to a surprised Michael and Scott.

"We thought we could not continue to fight LOEP if they know who we were. So we designed these," Nina said triumphantly. "So what do you think?"

Michael and Scott stood there in surprise. After one minute Scott spoke.

"It's a good idea," Scott commented. "LOEP will never know what hit them."

"Have you created secret names?" Michael asked.

"I'm Velocity." James said triumphantly. Nina thought about the question. She then smiled and answered.

"I'm Tsunami," she said with pride.

"This is great," Scott announced. "Now you can fight LOEP without them knowing who you are."

"What about you?" James (Velocity) asked.

"I … I'd rather work alone." Scott answered.

"You should also make a costume," Nina (Tsunami) suggested.

"No." Scott answered. "I want LOEP to know when I attack them." Scott started to grow angry. Velocity saw this and quickly changed the subject.

"I've finished the walkie-talkie system," he announced. Everyone faced Velocity. Velocity took four small headphones out of his pocket. He handed everyone a headphone. He then explained how to use the headphones.

"It's simple," Velocity said. "Tap the microphone once to talk to Michael, twice to talk to me, three times to talk to Tsunami, and four times to talk to Scott. Michael looked at his headphone. He noticed the number "1" engraved on it. He looked at Scott's. It had the number "4" engraved on it. Michael guessed everyone had a number engraved on their headphone according to the number of taps it took to contact them.

"Never tap your own number," Velocity ordered. He smiled. "You will barely be able to see those headphones once they are under your mask."

Michael smiled. He knew that the next time they fought LOEP, they were going to hit them harder than they had ever done before. Suddenly, Michael's smile disappeared.

"Did you see Shadow Paperboy?" Michael askcd. The room was suddenly silent.

"I saw him," Tsunami said.

"Me too," Velocity added.

"I … I don't know who he is. But he knows your weapons."

Scott stood up from Michael's bed." I've got to go," he said flatly.

"Where?" Michael asked.

"Home," Scott answered. "I have to finish my homework." Scott turned to leave.

"Scott," Michael called. Scott turned to face his brother. "Did you see Shadow Paperboy?" Michael asked.

Scott considered the question. "No," he answered finally.

With that, Scott left Michael, Velocity and Tsunami and went to his home.

Chapter 2

Gifts From Scizzorman

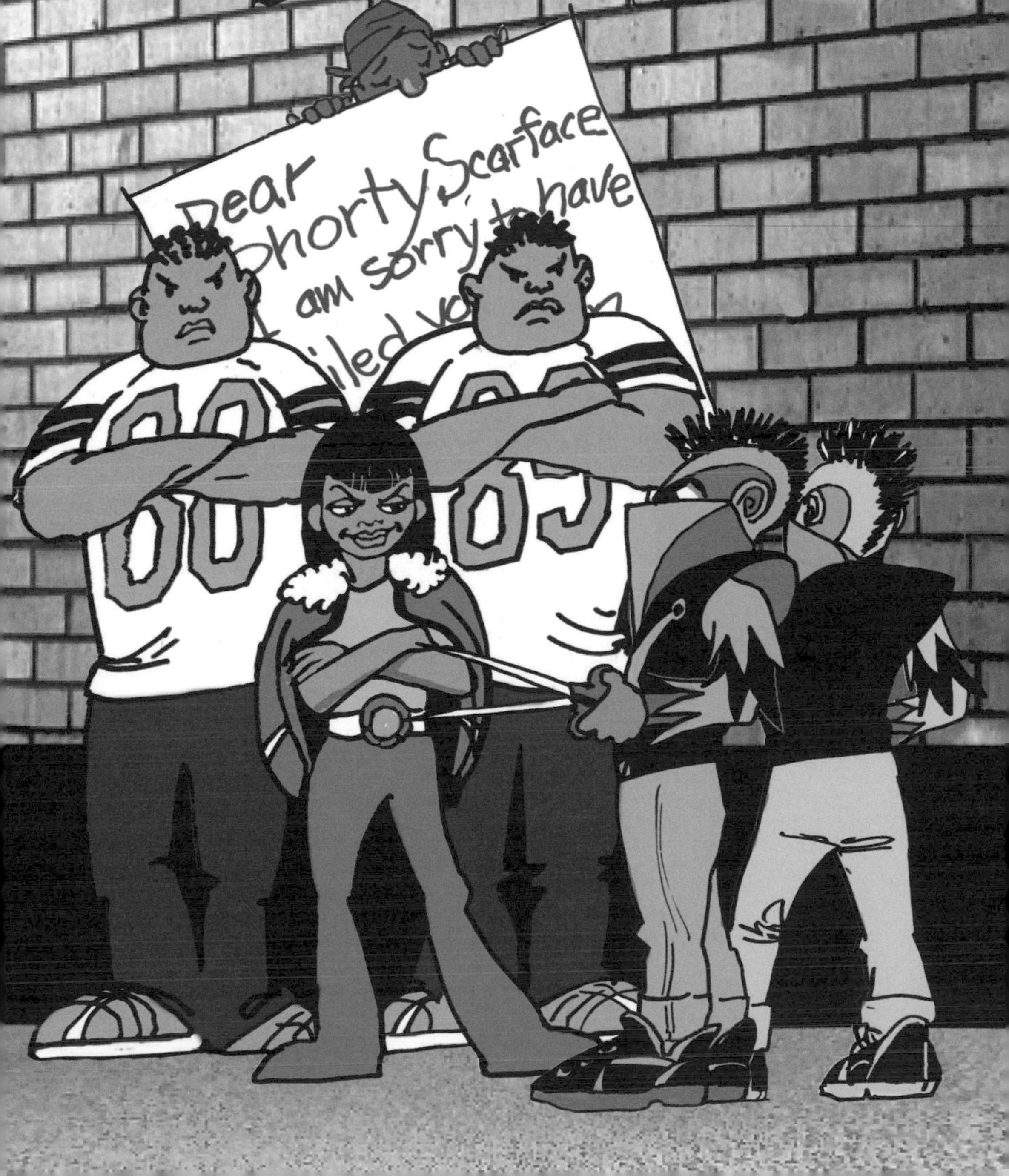

TWO

Later that day Shorty Scarface sat in the principal's office at P.S. 244 with Copycat. Copycat had recently been found in the basement in one of the prison rooms. Shorty Scarface was the only one in LOEP who had a master key. Once Shorty opened the door that held Copycat, he saw Copycat in a protractor trap. Shorty freed him and Copycat explained what had happened.

Now they sat in the principal's office trying to figure out a way to crush their enemies.

Shorty sighed.

"All my enemies have come together," he said. "They have come together to stand against me. We have tried to crush them but they have held their ground. If this continues, we will not gain control of P.S. 266."

"Then we have to turn to drastic measures," Copycat answered. Copycat and Shorty sat in silence for over a minute thinking. Suddenly, Copycat's eyes lit up. He had an idea.

"Let's send all the bullies from downtown and all the bullies from P.S. 244 to take over P.S. 266!" he suggested. Shorty looked at him questioningly.

"Paperboy, James, Nina and Scott never defeated the army of bullies you had ordered to catch them. They ran away. They could not handle so many bullies. They were overwhelmed. So what would happen if we sent more than five times that amount of bullies to P.S. 266? Nobody would be able to defend anything against such a force. If we can do this, we will easily gain control of P.S. 266."

"That idea is crazy." Shorty remarked. "Do you realize if all the bullies are defeated LOEP will fall?"

"Yes," Copycat answered. "But that could not possibly happen! We have thousands of bullies! Think about it. It would be like a war. Except the enemy would stand no chance of winning. They won't even know we have planned to attack them until it's too late. There will be little resistance against our force."

Shorty smiled. " War," he repeated slowly. "I like it, I like it a lot. But it's too risky. I like it, but I won't do it."

Copycat sighed, "Forget it then."

"Go to the playground," Shorty ordered. "Another tournament will be starting soon." Copycat smiled and exited the principal's office.

Meanwhile, a girl and two boys reached the entrance to P.S. 244. The girl opened the door and the two boys stepped inside. Two bullies stood on each side of the hallway. Once they saw the girl and the two boys, they took out their scissor guns and aimed. One bully walked in front of the girl.

"Who are you?" he asked. The bully looked at the girl who appeared to be about 12 years old. She was light skinned and had long, dark hair. She seemed to be about 4 feet tall. He then looked at the two boys. The boys looked like monsters. They were both more than 6 ft. tall and had huge arms with muscles bulging out of them. They were both light skinned and seemed to be about 16 years old.

"I'm Lisa," the girl answered. Lisa then pointed to one of the boys. "This is Paul." She then pointed to the other. "And this is Peter."

"I'm in the second grade." Paul said proudly.

Lisa gave Paul a fierce look.

"Sorry, boss," Paul said softly.

"Are you a member?" the bully asked.

"Not exactly," Lisa answered. "We were sent here by ScizzorMan." (ScizzorMan is one of four identical quadruplets. The names of the other three brothers are ScizzorMan A, ScizzorMan B and ScizzorMan C. ScizzorMan was defeated by Paperboy in the first book.)

All the bullies gasped. Lisa smiled. "We would like to talk to Shorty Scarface." The bully eyed Lisa suspiciously. Lisa saw this and pulled a piece of paper from her pocket.

"Read this!" she ordered. The bully took the note from Lisa and read it as best as he could with his elementary school education.

"It's signed by ScizzorMan," the bully uttered. He looked at Lisa. "Fine." The bully turned to two other bullies. "Take them to the principal's office." The two bullies nodded and escorted Lisa, Paul and Peter to the principal's office. Once they were outside the office, one of the bullies knocked on the door. Suddenly, the other ScizzorMen appeared behind Lisa, Paul, Peter and the two bullies.

"Shorty Scarface is not to be disturbed right now." ScizzorMan C announced. "What do you want?"

"I have to speak to Shorty Scarface," Lisa said flatly. With a smile she added, " Right now!"

The two bullies who escorted Lisa, Paul and Peter left. Lisa turned and knocked on the door again. ScizzorMan A grabbed Lisa's shoulder and roughly turned her around.

"He's not to be disturbed!" he said in an angry tone. Lisa looked at ScizzorMan A's hand. She then removed it from her shoulder.

"Don't touch me," she warned. This enraged ScizzorMan A and his brothers. ScizzorMan A pulled out a scissor gun and aimed at Lisa. Lisa looked toward Paul and Peter.

"Get them!" she ordered.

Without hesitating, Paul knocked the scissor gun out of ScizzorMan A's hand, then using his heavy fist he punched ScizzorMan A. ScizzorMan A flew extremely hard into the wall, then slowly fell off the wall and to the floor. Paul had defeated ScizzorMan A with one blow.

ScizzorMan B took out his scissor gun, aimed and fired at Peter. The scissors hit Peter but did not hurt him. Peter grew angry. He jumped and landed hard on his feet. The floor shook and the remaining ScizzorMen lost their balance and fell. Peter and Paul walked to the ScizzorMen.

Suddenly, the door opened. Shorty Scarface stood at the door. Lisa's back was to Shorty. The first thing Shorty noticed was ScizzorMan B and C. He watched in surprise as Paul and Peter each picked up a ScizzorMan like a bag of flour, punched them and then swung them into the wall. Both ScizzorMen fell to the ground. Lisa smiled.

She turned around. She stepped back in surprise when she saw the door open and Shorty in front of it. Shorty stared at Lisa.

"Who are you?" he asked. Paul and Peter stood on either side of Lisa.

"We're gifts from ScizzorMan," Lisa said smiling. She handed the note to Shorty. Shorty read the note.

Dear Shorty Scarface,

I am sorry to have failed you. In compensation, I give to you a trio capable of taking over P.S. 266 by themselves. Their names are Lisa, Peter and Paul. This trio is very strong. With them P.S. 266 will be yours for the taking.

PS. Destroy Paperboy for me.

Signed,

ScizzorMan

Shorty looked at Lisa, Paul and Peter.

"Come inside," he offered.

The trio stepped inside as Shorty walked to the window. He turned to the trio.

"So ScizzorMan sent you to help LOEP take over P.S. 266," Shorty said. He smiled. "Maybe he's right. Nobody has ever defeated ScizzorMan so easily." He looked at the trio again.

"Do you want to be recruited into LOEP?" he asked.

"Oh yes," Lisa answered. "My heart is as cold as yours." Shorty looked at Lisa questioningly. Lisa quickly decided to change the subject.

"I'm Lisa," she said. She pointed to the boys beside her. "This is Peter and this is Paul."

"I'm in the second grade," Paul said proudly. Lisa turned angrily to him.

"Equilibrium!" she screamed.

" Ahhh!" Paul screamed in pain. He then fell to his knees clutching his head. Lisa turned back to a puzzled Shorty Scarface.

"Paul is allergic to big words," Lisa declared. Shorty blinked.

"As you can see," Lisa continued, " I am the brains of the

operation."

"I can tell," Shorty answered as he watched Peter pick his nose.

"Normally, I would just recruit you three and send you downstairs. But you three are special. I can use you here."

Suddenly, the two ScizzorMen who were beaten up walked inside the room rubbing their heads.

"ScizzorMen!" Shorty called. The ScizzorMen faced Shorty. "Give these three a room."

"In the basement?" ScizzorMan A asked angrily.

"No." Shorty answered. "Here."

"You recruited them?" ScizzorMan B asked in surprise and anger.

"We don't have any more rooms," ScizzorMan C retorted.

"Then you three are moving out of your rooms," Shorty answered.

"Where will we go?" ScizzorMan C asked.

"You figure it out. I still want to see you at P.S. 244 whether you have a place to sleep or not." The ScizzorMen gasped in surprise at Shorty.

"Your room now belongs to these three!" Shorty declared pointing to Lisa, Paul and Peter. He then turned to the ScizzorMen.

"Escort them to their rooms!" he ordered

In frustration, the ScizzorMen led the trio outside the principal's office. Once outside, ScizzorMan B grabbed Lisa's throat.

"You think you can just come in here one day and outshine us?" he asked. Peter grabbed ScizzorMan B's throat.

"Don't talk to the boss like that," he ordered. ScizzorMan B let go of Lisa and Peter in turn let go of ScizzorMan B.

"We're just too good," Lisa remarked.

"You're good for nothing!" ScizzorMan A screamed.

The argument between the trio and the ScizzorMen was interrupted as a bully ran frantically towards them.

"We are being attacked!" he screamed. " We're being ……."

Suddenly, a weapon struck the bully and he fell to the floor. Both the ScizzorMen and the trio gasped in horror as they saw the weapon that struck the bully.

A black paper blade boomerang.

Chapter 3

Unstoppable Enemies

THREE

The next day during class, Miss Rex went over the words she had given the class the day before. In other words, Michael's class was once again uneventful. Forty five minutes later the bell rang for recess. Michael went to the janitor's closet and changed. Paperboy walked out of the closet. He was armed with two paper airplanes, one on each hand between the pointer and middle finger, two PBB's, one on each hand between the middle and index finger, two paper lasers, one in each of his two front pockets, and two paper claws, one on each hand. Paperboy walked out to recess.

Outside he saw no bullies. Suddenly, Paperboy's walkie-talkie received static. James' voice came through.

"Michael," he said.

"Yeah," Michael answered.

"Some people are climbing the gate. I can't see them well from here. Go and check it out. Tsunami and I will be out soon."

"Alright," Paperboy answered through the walkie-talkie.

With that, Paperboy walked over to the gate. Once he got there he saw a girl and two boys climbing the gate. In thirty seconds, they were in the playground. It was the trio, Lisa, Paul and Peter. Lisa walked up to Paperboy.

"So you're Paperboy," she remarked. "We've been given orders to destroy you." Paperboy looked at Lisa.

"I can't let that happen," Paperboy replied. Lisa smiled.

"We are not going to fail. We never fail. We are going to destroy you." Lisa turned to Paul and Peter.

"Lisa!"

Lisa turned to see Velocity skating towards her. Tsunami ran behind him.

"What are you doing here?" Velocity asked.

"I don't know you," Lisa remarked. Velocity took off his mask, revealing his face. Lisa looked at James and gasped.

"James?" she asked. "Why are you here?"

"This is my new school. Why are you here?"

"I'm here ….."

"Not that I don't miss you." James interrupted. "It's just a little surprising for your best friend to suddenly appear at your school one day. Nina's here too." James excitedly pointed to Nina.

"Lisa?" Nina asked. "Is that really you?" Lisa nodded. Her face then turned serious. "I'm a member of LOEP now," she said calmly.

"What!" James exclaimed. "You can't work with them! You're not like them!"

"Yes, I am!" Lisa retorted. "How would you know? One day we were all playing, having fun, and the next day you're gone. You don't know who I am!" James stepped back in surprise at Lisa's rage.

"Now I am a member of LOEP and I have been ordered to destroy Paperboy."

"You may be right," James uttered. "Maybe I don't know everything about you, but I know this. You have a heart, Lisa. You care about people. You are not like those people in LOEP. You will never be like them."

Lisa just glared at James and turned to Paul and Peter.

"Destroy them all!" she ordered.

Without hesitation, Paul went up to Paperboy and punched him with his heavy fist. Paperboy flew 5 feet back. The attack was so powerful that Paperboy dropped one of his PBB's. Peter went up to James and grabbed him. He then swung James to the gate. James hit the gate, bounced off and fell to the floor. Tsunami fired the water pen at Peter. Peter blocked the water with his hand and approached Tsunami.

"Oh no," Tsunami uttered.

After thirty seconds, Paperboy stood up. He fired a PBB at Paul. The PBB hit Paul but barely hurt him. Paul stared angrily at the paper cut Paperboy had given him. He walked to Paperboy. Paperboy ran towards Paul and attacked him with his paper airplanes. Paul ignored the attack and grabbed Paperboy. Instinctively, Paperboy pierced Paul with his

Paper claw. Paul also ignored this attack and began choking Paperboy.

"Paper cuts are not working," Paperboy thought, horrified.

After about ten seconds, James stood up. He looked at Peter. Peter had grabbed Tsunami and punched her. Tsunami fell five feet back. James then faced Paul who was choking the life out of Paperboy. He turned to Lisa.

"Lisa," he called desperately, "Stop this."

"Leave me alone," Lisa said curtly.

Suddenly Peter grabbed James.

"Hey," he shouted, "You don't sp...spoke to the boss unless your told to."

He swung James away from Lisa. Paperboy watched as James hit the ground. He was afraid that would be the last thing he would ever see. Paperboy squirmed as death's shadow slowly engulfed him. If Paul did not stop choking him soon, he was going to die. Suddenly, a dark figure kicked Paul's leg. Paul dropped Paperboy and faced the dark figure. It was Shadow Paperboy. Shadow Paperboy desperately threw a PBB at Paul. The PBB hit but barely hurt Paul. Shadow Paperboy then helped a greatly weakened Paperboy up.

"Follow me!" he instructed.

Paperboy followed Shadow Paperboy to his Papermobile.

"Get out of here." he ordered.

"Wait," Paperboy said. He tapped on his walkie talkie four times to contact Scott.

"Scott?" Paperboy asked. "Scott, are you there?" Paperboy watched curiously as Shadow Paperboy touched his ear. He then quickly put his head down.

"Go!" he ordered. Shadow Paperboy ran back to the playground. Paperboy watched as Shadow Paperboy ran to Velocity. Velocity got up and spotted Shadow Paperboy.

"Skate out of here!" he ordered.

"Who are you?" James asked. James reached for Shadow Paperboy's mask. Shadow Paperboy grabbed James' hand trying his best not to pierce him with his paper claw.

"Go," Shadow Paperboy said again.

He ran to Peter, who had just grabbed Tsunami. Paul spotted Shadow Paperboy and ran to him. Velocity saw this and threw a protractor at Paul. Before Paul turned around, Velocity skated as fast as he could to Paperboy. Paul turned around to face his attackers, but nobody was there. Puzzled, Paul looked up at the sky. Nobody was there either. He looked down at his shirt. Nobody was there either. Frantically looking for his attackers, Paul took off his shoe and looked inside. Nobody was there.

"Where did they go?" Paul asked himself.

Paperboy and James watched as Tsunami was thrown to the ground. Peter picked her up. Suddenly, Shadow Paperboy kicked Peter. Peter dropped Tsunami and reached for Shadow Paperboy. Shadow Paperboy moved out of Peter's grasp and quickly helped Tsunami up.

"Go!" he commanded.

Without hesitation, Tsunami ran to Paperboy and James.

"Let's go!" she exclaimed.

Paperboy unlocked his bike and rode out of P.S. 266. Tsunami ran after him. Velocity skated after her.

Meanwhile, Shadow Paperboy threw a black PBB at Peter. Peter angrily grabbed Shadow Paperboy and started choking him.

"They're escaping!" Lisa exclaimed.

"Huh?" Peter asked. Peter released Shadow Paperboy who quickly ran away.

"They left the school!" Lisa exclaimed. "Get them."

"Okay, boss." Peter replied. He ran out the school. Lisa hastily ran to Paul who was still hopelessly searching for his attackers.

"Paul!" she screamed. Paul faced Lisa. "Follow Peter."

"But boss, I'm looking for somebody."

"Follow Peter!"

Paul ran to Peter. Peter stood outside the school. Lisa caught up with them.

"They're gone, boss," Peter said. Lisa lowered her head in disgust. "We'll have to go back then. Shorty's not going to like this." A very small smile appeared on Lisa's face. "But the ScizzorMen will."

Lisa, Paul and Peter started their walk back to P.S. 244. James's words still haunted Lisa.

"You will never be like them."

In desperation, Lisa turned to Paul and Peter.

"Guys?" she asked. "Can you keep a secret?"

"Sure boss," Peter answered. "I can keep a secret very well. Why, I could tell you five secrets I've been keeping for people." Peter said proudly.

"He sounds trustworthy to me." Paul commented. Lisa stared at Paul and Peter in disbelief.

"Never mind," she said. Lisa, Paul and Peter continued to walk to P.S. 244.

"James is wrong," Lisa said to herself. "He doesn't know me. Maybe he used to, but not anymore. I'm just as evil as everyone else in LOEP. And when I see Paperboy again, I'll prove it to him."

Chapter 4

Paperboy vs. Shadow Paperboy

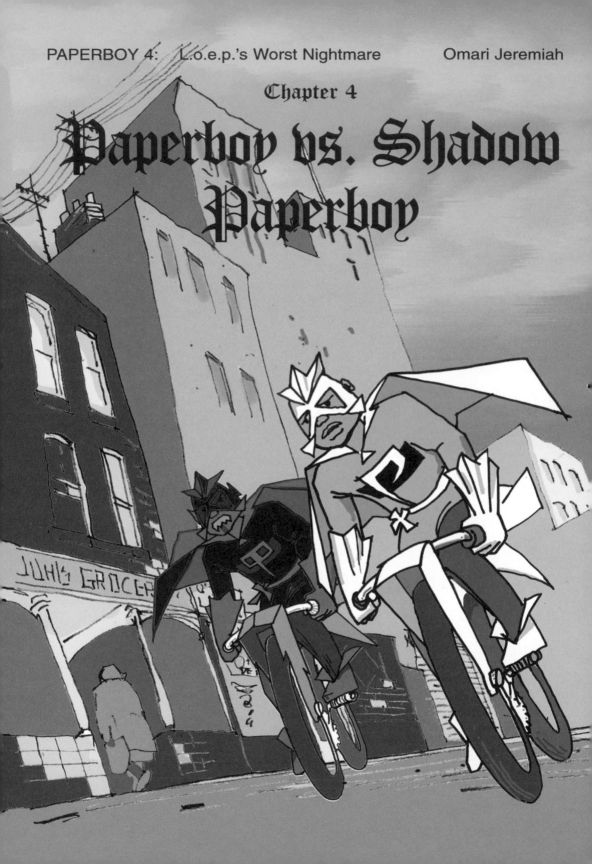

FOUR

After five minutes of walking the trio reached P.S. 244. They went inside and to the principal's office. Shorty Scarface, Copycat and the ScizzorMen were in the office. Shorty turned to face Lisa.

"Well?" he asked.

"They got away." Lisa said sadly. Shorty angrily punched the desk. Without concentrating, Shorty had actually punched a hole in the desk. The ScizzorMen smiled.

"You see, Shorty Scarface, we had them. We were winning. Then all of a sudden a black figure appeared. He fought Paul and Peter off and let Paperboy escape."

"Shadow Paperboy." Copycat said smiling. "It was him. He's been here too. He's attacked our bullies."

"Another enemy," Shorty said angrily. "I'm disappointed in you, Lisa."

"Max," Copycat said sarcastically, "War!"

Shorty Scarface thought about the idea of war that Copycat had suggested to him. He sighed. "Maybe," he answered.

He then turned to the trio.

"Get out!" he said curtly. Lisa, Paul and Peter left the principal's office. Shorty turned to Copycat.

"If I decided to go with your plan, how long would it take to prepare for war?"

Copycat thought about the question. "One week," he finally answered.

"War," Shorty repeated. Every time he said it, the idea sounded better and better.

Meanwhile, Paperboy, Velocity and Tsunami had just arrived at Paperboy's house. Paperboy took off his mask and opened the door. Michael, Velocity and Tsunami then walked to his room. Once in his room, Tsunami took off her mask. Michael collapsed on his bed.

"What a day." Tsunami exclaimed.

"Alright," Velocity said angrily. "We have to find out who Shadow Paperboy is. I can't take it anymore. Whoever he is……"

"It's Scott" Michael said sadly. Velocity and Tsunami turned to Michael.

"How do you know?" Tsunami asked.

"Think about it." Michael said. "Shadow Paperboy knows all my weapons and how to use them. We haven't seen Scott for a while. Plus, when I tried to contact Scott in front of Shadow Paperboy, Shadow Paperboy touched his ear as if receiving what I said through the walkie-talkie."

Michael closed his eyes. "But why? Why is he separating himself from us? Why won't he tell me?"

"You're jumping to conclusions." Velocity said. "It may be just coincidence."

"What about Lisa?" Tsunami asked.

"Lisa's crazy." Velocity said angrily. "Both she and I know she does not belong in LOEP. I don't know why she joined. Is she trying to prove something? And being with those two monsters that not even a doctor would call boys?" Velocity's voice rose. "I remember. She told me she wanted to be a doctor. How is joining LOEP related to becoming a doctor? What is she thinking? What is she ...."

"Calm down," Tsunami interrupted.

"We all went to P.S. 255. Lisa was such a nice girl. Maybe you and I moved to another school, but there is no way Lisa could have changed so drastically. No way"

Michael thought about Scott being Shadow Paperboy but after about five minutes, sleep overtook him.

The next day Michael got out of bed. He looked around his room. Velocity and Tsunami had left. Michael did his normal morning routine and then walked to class and took his seat.

"Test time!" Miss Rex announced. The class groaned. Michael gasped. He had not studied for the test. But because he had listened very well in class, the test was not very difficult. Forty five minutes later, the bell rang. The test was over.

Michael handed in his test and raced to the janitor's closet. Paperboy walked out. He was armed with the same amount of weapons as the day before. Outside, Paperboy saw no bullies. Suddenly, he saw Scott climbing the gate.

"Scott!" Paperboy exclaimed. Paperboy ran to Scott. When he got there Scott was in the playground.

"Scott," Paperboy exclaimed, "It's nice to see you." Then, in a more serious voice, Paperboy added, "I have to talk to you."

"No time." Scott prepared to run. Paperboy grabbed him. "Scott, I know you are Shadow Paperboy."

Scott turned around. "Am I?" he asked.

"I figured it out," Paperboy replied.

Scott smiled. His smile then faded. "I have to go!" he said. He then ran towards P.S. 266. Paperboy tapped his walkie-talkie four times to contact him. But before he could say anything, Scott entered P.S. 266.

Suddenly, Paperboy felt a kick. The kick was so hard that he crumpled to the ground. He slowly stood up and faced his attacker. He gasped. It was Shadow Paperboy!

Shadow Paperboy grabbed Paperboy.

"I'm going to destroy you," he said. Paperboy looked in horror as

Shadow Paperboy attacked him with his paper airplanes.

"You're not Scott." Paperboy said. Shadow Paperboy ignored this and grabbed Paperboy and swung him to the gate. Paperboy hit the gate, bounced off and hit the ground. He then got up and looked at Shadow Paperboy.

"Who are you?" Paperboy asked. "One day you save my life and the next day you try to destroy me." Without answering, Shadow Paperboy attacked with his paper airplanes. Paperboy dodged the attack.

"I don't want to fight you." Paperboy answered.

"You are going to pay for all you have done to me!" Shadow Paperboy roared. Suddenly Shadow Paperboy's back was splashed with water. He turned around to face Tsunami. Shadow Paperboy noticed a protractor trap behind Tsunami. He kicked Tsunami into the protractor trap.

"No!" Tsunami screamed.

"That's it," Paperboy said. "Nobody does that to my friend. I'm going to defeat you." Shadow Paperboy turned as Paperboy attacked him with his paper airplane. Shadow Paperboy retaliated with a hard kick. Paperboy fell to the ground. Suddenly, Velocity skated to Shadow Paperboy and attacked with his protractors. Shadow Paperboy dodged the attack, grabbed Velocity with his paper claw, and swung him as far as he could. Velocity fell seven feet back. He landed hard on the ground. A school guard stood ten feet away from the fight, watching carefully.

31

"Guard 1 to Raptor," the school guard said through his walkie-talkie. "Still fighting, waiting for the perfect moment."

"Keep up the good work," a voice replied through the walkie-talkie. "Remember, wait until he is on the ground for a while. That way he won't struggle." The school guard nodded as he watched.

Paperboy threw a PBB at Shadow Paperboy. Shadow Paperboy also threw a PBB at Paperboy. The two PBB's collided and fell to the ground. Shadow Paperboy grabbed Paperboy with one hand and attacked mercilessly with his paper airplane. He did this for about two minutes, attacking Paperboy every two seconds. He then swung Paperboy to the gate. Paperboy hit the gate and bounced off. But before he could fall, Shadow Paperboy punched Paperboy with all his strength.

Paperboy forcefully hit the gate, bounced off and fell to the floor. This was more than Paperboy could take. Paperboy could barely lift a finger. Shadow Paperboy stepped back. Suddenly, protractors pierced Shadow Paperboy's feet and ropes came out of them, binding Shadow Paperboy's body tightly. He was caught in a protractor trap. Shadow Paperboy fell to the ground. Velocity appeared in back of Shadow Paperboy.

"Run!" he ordered. As hard as it was, Paperboy painfully got to his feet and ran to his Papermobile.

"Noooooo!" Shadow Paperboy screamed. Using all of his remaining strength, he tried to break free from the protractor trap. Slowly, the ropes cut away. After one minute, Shadow Paperboy was free from the trap. He threw a black PBB at Velocity and watched him hit the ground. He then watched as Paperboy rode his Papermobile out of P.S. 266.

"This is not over," Shadow Paperboy whispered.

Paperboy painfully pedaled down the street, away from P.S. 266. In five minutes, he would be home. He had a lot of healing and thinking to do.

"Whoever Shadow Paperboy is, he's a fierce fighter," Paperboy thought. "Even with my weapons, he's a better fighter than I am."

Suddenly, another bike rode beside Paperboy. Paperboy could not believe who was riding the bike. It was Shadow Paperboy!

"This is not over!" Shadow Paperboy screamed. He rammed his bike into the Papermobile. Paperboy and the Papermobile went flying into the sidewalk hitting the pavement extremely hard. Shadow Paperboy loomed over him.

"Before I destroy you," he said. "Let's see your real face!" Shadow Paperboy angrily took off Paperboy's mask. He gasped at the sight of Michael.

"Oh no," Shadow Paperboy said putting Paperboy's mask back on.

"No, Nooo. This can't be."

Shadow Paperboy stepped back in horror. He rode his bike away from Paperboy. Paperboy managed to spot a school guard nearby.

"We got him," the school guard announced through his walkie-talkie.

After that Paperboy reluctantly slipped into unconsciousness.

Chapter 5
Tsunami's Rescue

FIVE

Five minutes later, Velocity managed to get back on his feet. He saw Tsunami who was still caught in the protractor trap. Velocity skated over to the protractor trap. He cut the ropes with another protractor and took two protractors out of Tsunami's foot.

"Are you okay?" Velocity asked.

"I'm fine," Tsunami answered. "But what about Michael? Is he okay?"

"I don't know," Velocity answered. Velocity tapped on his walkie talkie once.

"Michael! Michael are you there? Michael? Please answer Michael?" Velocity lowered his head in defeat. "It's not like him to not answer the walkie-talkie." Tsunami then gasped.

"Look," she ordered. Velocity turned around to see a school guard carrying Paperboy.

"He's hurt badly," Velocity observed. Velocity turned to Tsunami. "Let's follow that school guard."

Tsunami stood up in agreement. "Let's go," she said.

Velocity and Tsunami secretly followed the school guard into P.S. 266. The school guard walked down two hallways and turned a corner.

Velocity and Tsunami followed quietly. The school guard walked halfway down the hallway. Next he stopped at a door. He took out a key, opened the door then closed the door behind him. Velocity looked at Tsunami.

"What now?" she asked. Velocity thought about the question. He had an idea. Velocity set up a protractor trap right outside the door. He carefully knocked on the door, doing his best to avoid his own trap. He stepped back. Thirty seconds later, the door opened. A school guard stood at the door. But this was not the same school guard who had carried Paperboy.

"Why are you here?" the school guard asked. "And what's with the costumes?"

"We're lost," Velocity said pointing to Tsunami. "Could you help us find our way to the playground?"

"Well," the school guard said stepping outside with the door open. "It's …."

Suddenly, the school guard was caught in the protractor trap. He fell to the floor. Velocity and Tsunami walked past the school guard and into the room.

"Thanks for your help," Tsunami said sarcastically. She then closed the door.

Meanwhile, Paperboy had just regained consciousness. His eyes slowly opened. He was in an empty room. He still had all his weapons. Paperboy groaned. He was still very weak because Shadow Paperboy had nearly destroyed him. Paperboy stood up from the floor. Suddenly, the door opened. Mr. Raptor stepped into the room.

"Paperboy," he announced, "I've finally caught you."

Paperboy stood in shock looking at his father.

"You know Shadow Paperboy?" Paperboy said surprised.

"No," Mr. Raptor said. "I don't know Shadow Paperboy. But I wish I did. Without him I would not have caught you." Mr. Raptor slowly walked to Paperboy.

"You may have escaped me in the past, but now I've got you. Before this day is over, I will know your true identity."

"Why have you been trying to capture me?" Paperboy asked.

"Because you are a menace to the school," Mr. Raptor answered. "You start fights in the playground and you hurt innocent students."

"I don't hurt students," Paperboy uttered. "I defend them. There's an organization of bullies that wants to take over this school. The name of the organization is LOEP, which stands for League of Evil People. I've been defending the school from that organization."

"You're a liar!" Mr. Raptor screamed. "I won't believe anything that you say." Mr. Raptor was now within arms reach of Paperboy. He grabbed Paperboy. Paperboy instinctively pierced him with his paper claw.

"AAHH!" Mr. Raptor cried out in pain. He looked at Paperboy.

"You're going to pay for that," he said angrily.

Meanwhile, Velocity and Tsunami had found a stairway that went down. They walked down the stairway. The stairway led them to several doors similar to the basement of P.S. 266. Velocity gasped. He turned to Tsunami.

"This is the basement of P.S. 266,"he uttered.

"Where do we start?" he asked Tsunami. Tsunami tapped her walkie-talkie once.

"Michael?" she asked. She heard static.

"Yeah," a weak voice answered back. Tsunami sighed in relief.

"Are you okay?" Tsunami asked.

"Yeah," Michael said, "But not for long. Mr. Raptor's here. He's trying ….he's trying to take off …..my …mask!"

Tsunami gasped. "Which room are you in?" she asked.

"I don't know," Paperboy replied. "Where are you?"

"In the basement," Tsunami replied. "There are a lot of doors here. It looks like the basement of P.S. 244."

"Are all the doors closed?"

"Yeah," Tsunami replied.

"I hope I'm close to you. Look for the door that's about to open.

That's the room I'm in."

Tsunami looked frantically at the doors. Suddenly a door opened.

"Let's go!" Tsunami ordered Velocity. He followed Tsunami to the open door.

Meanwhile, Paperboy did his best to protect himself from Mr. Raptor, who had just opened the door. Suddenly, Mr. Raptor punched Paperboy. Paperboy fell to the floor. He could not handle another fight. Shadow Paperboy had greatly weakened him. Plus, Paperboy could not bear to fight his own father.

"I guess the only way to accomplish my goal is to play by your rules," Mr. Raptor said surly. "You're a mystery, Paperboy. First you attack students, then you start talking to yourself. But fortunately, some mysteries can be solved."

"I wasn't talking to myself," Paperboy replied weakly.

Paperboy stood up. Mr. Raptor punched him again much harder than the first time. Paperboy hit the floor with a thud.

"Ohhhh" he groaned. Mr. Raptor stood over him. "Now, let's see who you really are." Mr. Raptor reached for Paperboy's mask. As he was about to unmask Paperboy, a blast of water hit his back. He turned around angrily. He saw Tsunami outside the door. "He's coming with me," Tsunami announced.

Mr. Raptor reached for his walkie-talkie and spoke through it.

"All school guards to the basement," he ordered.

Tsunami fired the water pen at Mr. Raptor's face.

"Ahhhhh!" Mr. Raptor screamed. Suddenly, Velocity skated into the room, grabbed Paperboy and helped him to his feet. Paperboy and Velocity ran out the room. Tsunami followed them. Mr. Raptor wiped water from his face.

"Come back here!" he screamed. But he was too late. Velocity, Tsunami and Paperboy raced up the stairway. Tsunami opened the door and allowed Paperboy and Velocity to get out. She exited the door and closed it.

"School guards are coming!" Tsunami shouted. Velocity skated to another nearby door. He opened the door. Tsunami and Paperboy ran inside. Velocity closed the door.

"We'll be safe in here," he declared.

"No, we won't," Paperboy said weakly.

"Of course we will," Tsunami said. "All the school guards are going to the basement."

"Look," Paperboy said pointing. Tsunami looked to where Paperboy was pointing. She could not believe whom she saw. It was the Mad Hunter! The Mad Hunter glared at them.

"Not yet," he said. "I will destroy everyone in P.S. 266. This way I can easily get to and destroy my prey." The Mad Hunter ran to Paperboy and raised his fist. Before anyone could do anything, the Mad Hunter struck. Paperboy fell to the ground. He was knocked out cold. The Mad Hunter then tripped Velocity and once again raised his fist.

"No!" Tsunami screamed. She ran to the Mad Hunter. The Mad Hunter kicked her to the side and struck Velocity. Velocity was also knocked out cold. The Mad Hunter turned to Tsunami. He raised his fist.

"Soon, I will destroy you and everyone else," He struck her. Tsunami was knocked out cold like Paperboy and Velocity.

"But not yet," he added. With all three heroes knocked out, the Mad Hunter turned around and continued constructing his traps.

Meanwhile, Scott walked cautiously out to the playground. He looked around. No Shadow Paperboy. Scott smiled and quickly ran back into P.S. 266. He went into the janitor's closet. Copycat then ran out of the janitor's closet and out of P.S. 266. He frantically ran to P.S. 244. Once there, he ran inside the building. He ran past several bullies on his way to the principal's office. Once outside the office, he opened the door and stepped in. Inside were Shorty Scarface and the ScizzorMen. Copycat ran to Shorty Scarface, completely out of breath.

Shorty looked at him with a puzzled look. A minute later, Copycat caught his breath.

"I had to get here as fast as I could," he said breathlessly. "I had to tell you."

"Tell me what?" Shorty asked. Copycat smiled.

"I know Shadow Paperboy's true identity," he said with an evil grin.

Chapter 6

Shadow Is Brought To Light

SIX

Two hours later, Paperboy opened his eyes. He was still in the same room in which the Mad Hunter had knocked him out. He looked around the room. The Mad Hunter was not there. Paperboy spotted Velocity and Tsunami lying near him. He watched as Velocity and Tsunami groaned and opened their eyes. They both looked around the room.

Velocity stood up. "Is everyone okay?" he asked.

"Yeah," Paperboy and Tsunami answered in unison. Tsunami stood up and reached for the door.

"No," Paperboy said weakly. "It's too dangerous if we go back out like this. We have to take off our costumes and masks."

"Good idea," Velocity agreed. Paperboy, Velocity and Tsunami removed their costumes and masks and put them in their knapsacks. Nina opened the door. Michael, James and Nina stepped out. They walked out of P.S. 266 and to Michael's house. On the way, Michael picked up his battered Papermobile. Michael's mother and Scott were waiting when they arrived.

"Where were you?" Michael's mother asked. Michael thought about the question.

"School," he finally answered.

"Doing a science project," James added.

Michael's mother nodded. "Okay. But next time tell me, please tell me you will be coming home late. I was worried about you."

Michael nodded.

Michael, James and Nina went to Michael's room. Michael collapsed on the bed. He had had a very bad day. He was attacked by Shadow Paperboy, captured by Mr. Raptor and knocked out by the Mad Hunter.

"What a day!" Nina sighed.

James sighed also. "Everything went wrong," he said. He angrily added, "And we still don't know who Shadow Paperboy is!"

Suddenly, Scott entered the room.

"Where have you been?" Nina asked with a voice filled with anger. "We have been looking for you for a while."

Scott looked sadly at Nina. "I'm sorry," he said. "I'm so sorry." Tears started flowing down his eyes.

"What's wrong?" Michael asked.

Scott wiped tears from his eyes and looked at Michael. "Everything happened so fast. I didn't know."

Michael looked at Scott in horror.

"Scott," Michael said trembling, "Are you Shadow Paperboy?"

"The name is not Shadow Paperboy," Scott replied. "It's

Nightmare."

"It was you?" Michael said in surprise and anger. "You were Shadow Paperboy all the time?"

"The name is Nightmare," Scott said raising his voice.

"The name doesn't matter!" Michael roared. "You attacked me!"

"I know," Scott said, tears in his eyes. "I'm sorry. But at the time, I didn't know it was you. The whole thing started when I was at P.S. 244 that morning. Copycat had changed into Paperboy. I chased Copycat out of P.S. 244, determined to destroy him once and for all. Copycat ran to P.S. 266 and towards the gate. All of a sudden about ten bullies attacked me and blocked my view of Copycat. I defeated them all and then spotted Paperboy close to the gate. I climbed the gate and attacked you, thinking you were Copycat. I did not find out what a big mistake I made until I removed your mask. I was certain I would see Jason's face, but instead I saw yours. This surprised me. I then realized the total mistake I had made."

"Wait," Michael, said. "If you were Shadow Paperboy all along, then how did I talk to you and soon afterwards I was attacked by Shadow Paperboy?"

Scott thought about the question.

"It must have been Copycat," he said. "He probably changed into me while I was fighting those bullies."

"What did you tell him?" Scott asked.

Michael gasped as he remembered. "I told him Scott was Shadow Paperboy."

Scott stared at him in disbelief.

"How could you!" he roared. Michael lowered his head in defeat. Scott walked to Michael. "Do you know why I decided to become Nightmare? Or as you would say, Shadow Paperboy?"

Michael said nothing.

"I became Nightmare so I could get revenge on LOEP. I wanted Max and all the other members of LOEP destroyed. I knew I could not do this as Scott, so I decided to make a costume and mask to disguise myself. Your weapons were more efficient than any other weapon so I decided to copy all your weapons and color them black." Scott smiled a little. "It matched with the costume."

"I also renamed the weapons. Instead of the Papermobile, my bike is the Terrormobile. My black paper lasers are called terror lasers. My black paper airplanes are called terror planes, and my black paper blade boomerangs are called Terror Blade Boomerangs (TBB). And of course, my black Paper Claw is called the Terror Claw."

Scott's smiled faded. "And you tell one of my greatest enemies my secret identity?"

"This is pitiful," Michael replied. "You hate LOEP so much that you can't even think straight. You only became Shadow Paperboy so you could get revenge on LOEP. Scott, Listen to me carefully. You cannot defeat LOEP by yourself. You need us!" Michael looked at his brother. "Trust me, Scott, I've tried. It is just not possible. We have to work together."

"I don't need you!" Scott roared. "You don't understand, Michael. You'll never understand. LOEP took away everything I cared about. They took away my school. They made me a prisoner of my own school. Do you know what that's like? Of course you don't. You don't know anything."

"Sooner of later, you're going to fail, Scott. LOEP will catch you and nobody will be there to help you. You can't do this alone, Scott. Let us help you."

"I should have known," Scott said sadly. "I should have known you wouldn't understand. I should have never told you the truth. I should have never rescued you. I should have destroyed you." Tears streamed down Scott's face.

"You don't mean that," Michael, said confidently. Scott angrily turned and got ready to leave.

"Scott," Michael called. Scott stopped. "I thought we could trust each other. You could have told me the truth before."

Scott turned around and said. "Obviously, we can't trust each other."

He started to leave then stopped and looked at Michael.

"By the way, Nightmare is going to P.S. 244 tomorrow. And he is going to destroy LOEP. Alone." Scott exited Michael's room. Michael turned to James and Nina. Both James and Nina's mouths were agape as they stared at Michael. Michael sighed.

"All we can hope now is that Scott knows what he is doing," Michael said sadly.

Meanwhile, Shorty Scarface had just been told the secret identity of Shadow Paperboy by Copycat. He ordered Copycat and 20 bullies to guard the school's entrance. He ordered the trio and the ScizzorMen to stay inside the principal's office.

"What are you going to do?" a bully asked Shorty. Shorty smiled at the question.

"I'm going to settle unfinished business," he replied in an evil tone.

Chapter 7
The Favor Is Returned

SEVEN

The next day Michael got out of bed. He gently rubbed his head. He had not fully recovered from everything that had happened to him the day before. Michael was also worried about his brother. He knew nobody could defeat LOEP alone. He just hoped that Scott would soon realize this and let him and the others help him.

With that in mind, Michael took his shower, got dressed, had breakfast and changed into his Paperboy costume. Paperboy rode his battered Papermobile to P.S. 266 and did his usual routine. He was surprised to see the Terrormobile close by. He ran into the janitor's closet and changed. Michael walked to his classroom. Miss Rex was going over the test the class had taken. Forty-five minutes later, the bell rang for recess. Michael quickly walked out of class and to the janitor's closet where he changed.

Paperboy walked out of the janitor's closet fully armed with all his weapons. He walked to the playground. He saw no bullies. He saw Velocity in a hidden corner of the playground. He also saw Tsunami talking to her friends.

Suddenly, Nightmare (Shadow Paperboy) ran out of another corner of the playground. Paperboy watched as Nightmare unlocked the Terrormobile and rode away. Paperboy tapped his walkie-talkie four times.

"Scott," he called.

"What!" Scott answered.

"Don't do this," Paperboy begged. "Please."

"Leave me alone," Scott said curtly through the walkie-talkie. Paperboy put his hands down in defeat.

Nightmare continued riding the Terrormobile to P.S. 244. With one hand, Nightmare touched his ear. He thought about getting rid of the walkie-talkie but Michael's words ran through Nightmare's mind.

"You can't do this alone." Nightmare thought about this brother's words. He then began to wonder if Michael was right.

"No," Nightmare uttered. "I don't need anyone. I can do this alone."

But deep down in his sub-conscious mind, Michael's words still haunted him.

With these two opposing thoughts in mind, Scott rode up to P.S. 244. He leaned the Terrormobile against the school's wall. He hoped it would be there when he came back. Nightmare sighed deeply. He walked to the entrance of his old school and opened the door. Inside, he saw ten bullies on each side of the hallway. Nightmare prepared for the bullies to take out their scissor guns.

But instead of taking out their scissor guns, the bullies charged Nightmare. Nightmare attacked one bully with the terror airplane. The bully fell to the ground. Nightmare picked up the bully and threw him into the other nine bullies. All the bullies fell to the floor.

One bully got up and ran to Nightmare with his arm extended as if to punch Nightmare. Nightmare stepped back to avoid the attack. He quickly ran to the bully, grabbed his arm and swung him into the other bullies who had started to get up. All the bullies fell to the floor again.

Nightmare looked down the hallway. Suddenly, Jason turned the corner. He was not dressed as anybody. Jason walked to Nightmare.

"Shadow Paperboy, you've finally come. We've been expecting you, Scott."

"You escaped me and made me attack Paperboy," Nightmare said angrily. "Not to mention the horrible things you and the other bullies did to me when I was a prisoner."

"Yes," Jason recalled. "I enjoyed that. And I am going to enjoy doing it again when you're a prisoner once more."

"That will never happen!" Nightmare roared. Nightmare charged Jason. Once he was close enough, Nightmare attacked Jason fiercely with his terror airplanes.

"Ahhhh!" Jason cried out in pain as he fell to the ground.

Nightmare took out his terror laser. "Take this!" he screamed angrily. Nightmare mercilessly fired his terror lasers.

"Ahhhh!" Jason cried out once more.

Nightmare grabbed Jason with his terror claw. He swung Jason into a nearly wall. Jason hit the wall, bounced off and hit the floor.

"You're nothing unless you pretend to be someone else," Nightmare said as he watched Jason trying to stand up.

Jason smiled. "Is that all you got?" he taunted.

Nightmare threw a terror blade boomerang (TBB) at Jason. Jason fell to the floor once again.

He slowly got up and smiled again. "Soon, it's going to be all over, Scott." Nightmare looked at Jason.

"What are you talking about?" he asked.

"I'm talking about the end of P.S. 266," Jason replied. "Shorty hasn't agreed to it yet, but I can see it in his eyes. He likes the idea ….."

"What idea?"

"The idea of war," Jason said wickedly. "Soon all the bullies are going to come to P.S. 266 and take over the school. Nobody will be able to stop us. Not you, not Paperboy nor his friends. There will be too many. You were overwhelmed by a fraction of our bullies from P.S. 244. You will not stand a chance against all our bullies from P.S. 244 combined with all our bullies from downtown."

Nightmare stepped back in horror after hearing Jason's words.

"And the best part of it," Jason said with an evil smile on his face, "P.S. 266 won't be prepared for the attack at all."

"Unless I tell them," Nightmare replied.

"You won't be able to tell them,"

"Why not?"

"Because you will be here!" Jason said angrily. "You'll be a prisoner once again."

With that Nightmare ran to Jason and punched him with all his strength. Jason flew six feet back. He landed on the floor extremely hard.

"We'll see who stays and who leaves," Nightmare said rudely. He turned around. He gasped at who was behind him. It was Shorty Scarface! Shorty looked at Nightmare and smiled. He then ran around the corner.

"No," Nightmare roared as he ran to the end of the hallway and turned the corner. "You're not getting away!"

Jason watched as Nightmare ran after Shorty Scarface. He rubbed his head and smiled.

"Sometimes copying hurts," he said as he picked up a terror blade boomerang.

Nightmare continued to chase Shorty Scarface. He chased Shorty down a hallway. Shorty turned a corner. Two seconds later, Nightmare turned the corner also. After six minutes of this cat and mouse game, Nightmare screamed, "You can't get away from me!"

All of a sudden, Shorty turned another corner. Nightmare turned the same corner. But he did not see Shorty. Nightmare saw the giant doors that were in the hallway swing closed. Nightmare looked puzzled.

"What is going on?" he said to himself. Nightmare walked through the door and out to the playground. Outside there was nobody except Shorty Scarface. Little did Nightmare know that the ScizzorMen and the trio watched all the events from the principal's office. Nightmare walked to Shorty.

"It's over, Max," he said triumphantly. "LOEP is over. Once I defeat you, LOEP is basically destroyed."

Shorty chuckled. "You're probably right," he said with an evil smile. "But that won't happen. LOEP will live on forever. But if I were you, I wouldn't worry about LOEP right now, Shadow Paperboy, or should I say, Scott. I would worry about my survival." With that Shorty, took a sharp scissor from his pocket.

"What are you going to do with that?" Nightmare asked.

"I'm going to put a scar on your face," Shorty said. "I'm going to return the favor!"

"You still remember when I gave you that scar," Nightmare remarked.

"But you're not going to return any favor, Max. You're going to watch in horror as I pay you back for everything you've done to me. You're going to watch as I destroy you and your organization."

With that Nightmare attacked Shorty with his terror airplanes. Shorty back flipped and avoided the attack.

"You really want to fight?" Shorty howled. Shorty then took out a ruler. He looked at it. "You would do well as a member of LOEP. But too bad."

Nightmare angrily charged at Shorty. Once he was close enough, he attacked with his terror airplanes. Shorty blocked each attack with his ruler. He rolled behind Nightmare. Before, Nightmare could turn around, Shorty swung his ruler at Nightmare's lower back. Nightmare went flying five feet forward before hitting the ground.

Shorty walked toward him. Nightmare threw a TBB at him. The TBB hit Shorty's face. Shorty turned around and touched the paper cut on his face. Nightmare stood up. He looked at Shorty Scarface and then at the paper cut on his face.

"Is that a new look?" he asked.

Shorty glared at him. He charged at Nightmare. Once close enough, Shorty attacked with his ruler. Nightmare dodged the attack and grabbed Shorty's hand with his terror claw.

"It's over, Max."

With that Shorty whacked Nightmare's arm. Nightmare clutched his arm, the pain almost overwhelming him.

"Owww," he managed to say.

Shorty smiled. In one swift action, Shorty jabbed the ruler at Nightmare's chest, and turned completely around to face Nightmare while twisting the ruler at the same time. He struck Nightmare forcefully with the ruler. Shorty watched as Nightmare prepared to fall. He held the ruler in Nightmare's path. Nightmare fell on the ruler. Shorty pushed Nightmare back up with the ruler. Once Nightmare was back on his feet, Shorty punched him using a moderate amount of strength. Nightmare flew in the air. He hit the ground very, very hard. Shorty walked to him.

Nightmare painfully got back up. "No," he said. "I can't lose. I can't lose!"

Nightmare got up. Once Shorty was within reach, he threw another TBB at him. Shorty deflected the TBB with his ruler. Nightmare tried to attack Shorty with his terror airplane. Shorty blocked the attack. Nightmare continued to attack. Shorty continuously blocked the attacks with his ruler. He then counter attacked with a kick. Nightmare fell to the ground. Shorty picked him up and choked him with one hand while attacking him with the ruler in the other hand. He swung Nightmare seven feet away from him. Nightmare hit the ground hard.

"Ohhh," Nightmare groaned. He could barely lift a finger. Michael's words haunted him."You can't do this alone."

"I can do it," he said to himself.

Nightmare took out a terror laser and fired it. Shorty easily deflected the black paper balls with his ruler.

All of a sudden, it began to rain. Raindrops fell on Nightmare and his black paper weapons. Nightmare watched in horror as his terror airplanes and other weapons became wet and unusable.

"Oh no," Nightmare gasped. Nightmare dropped his now ineffective paper weapons. He also took off his mask. Shorty ran to Nightmare. When he was about five feet away from him, Shorty leaped three feet in the air going towards Nightmare with his ruler raised.

"Oh no," Nightmare roared. Shorty forcefully struck Nightmare as he came down. Once again, Nightmare hit the ground very hard. Shorty stood over Nightmare.

"It's time, Scott. It's time to return the favor." Nightmare slowly raised his arms in protest. Shorty whacked his arm with the ruler. Nightmare's arm painfully hit the ground. As Shorty took the scissor from his pocket, Nightmare remembered something. He quickly tapped his walkie-talkie.

"Michael," he said weakly

"Scott? Scott are you okay?" Paperboy answered through the walkie-talkie.

"You were right, Michael. I could not do this alone. I'm sorry. I'm sorry for what I said yesterday."

"Is something wrong?" Paperboy asked.

"I need your help," Nightmare said weakly as the scissor touched his face.

"Scott, what's wrong?"

Suddenly, Paperboy heard a loud scream through the walkie-talkie.

"Scott," Paperboy screamed. "No!"

Lisa had seen the whole thing and was very upset. She turned away from the window.

"Oh my," she said. "This is horrible." The ScizzorMen chuckled as they looked through the window.

"How could you watch that?" Lisa asked. "That guy never had a chance. I feel sorry for him."

"What do you mean you feel sorry for him? You're part of LOEP. You're supposed to be evil."

"Right," Lisa said. "I'm evil." Lisa suddenly did not like what she just said.

An hour later, Scott was in a room. He sadly touched the cut that was on his face. It would heal and leave a scar. He had failed. Shorty had defeated him and had returned the favor. But the worst thing was not either of these. The worst thing was Scott was a prisoner of P.S. 244 once again.

EIGHT

"Scott." Paperboy desperately screamed through his walkie-talkie. Paperboy tried to contact Scott many times but there was no response. School was now over. Paperboy, James and Nina walked towards Paperboy's house. Paperboy sighed and took off his mask in defeat.

"Something has happened to Scott," Michael said sadly. "I just hope he is okay."

"What was the last thing he said? James asked.

"He said he needed our help," Michael stated. "Then I heard a loud scream." James and Michael looked at each other sadly.

Michael, James and Nina reached Michael's house. Michael looked around. His mother was not home. Michael, James and Nina went to Michael's room. They all sat on his bed.

"We have to rescue Scott," he said.

"Michael," Nina said sadly, her head hanging low, "We might already be too late." Michael looked at Nina.

"But we can still try," Michael said tears in his eyes. "And hope we're not too late."

"Michael's right," James uttered. "We have to at least try."

Nina sighed. "I really don't want to go back there; bad memories. Nothing but bad memories."

"I understand," Michael replied warmly, "You don't have to go. Nobody has to go. I'll just have to sneak in …."

"Don't even think about it," James warned. "I don't really want to go back there either, but Scott's in trouble. He needs us. And I'm not going to let him down."

Nina turned to Michael. "James is right," she said. "I'm not going to let him down either."

Michael smiled a little. "Then let's come up with a plan. "Where would Scott be?" he asked.

"He should still be at P.S. 244," James answered.

"Then he would be in the basement under heavy guard," Nina said.

"That's the only place they would keep Scott," Nina agreed. She looked down. "If he's still alive."

Michael did his best to ignore Nina's comment. "I don't know where the basement is," he said.. He looked at James and Nina hopefully. They both shook their heads.

"Then how can we save Scott?" he asked. James and Nina thought about the question. Suddenly, Michael had a brilliant idea.

"I know what to do!" he said smiling.

Meanwhile, Scott looked sadly at his broken walkie-talkie. One of the bullies had discovered it in his ear, took it out and smashed it to pieces. Scott looked sadly at the door. Moments after that the door opened and the trio walked in. Lisa stood in front.

"We have news for you," she said. "In two hours you will be entering a tournament."

"No, I won't," Scott said forcefully. For a second, Lisa looked sadly at Scott. She then shook her head. Lisa had decided that she was indeed evil. She may not have liked the way it sounded, but she was part of LOEP. She had to be evil. Peter picked his nose as Lisa turned to leave.

"Soon, LOEP will be destroyed," Scott said. "And they'll be destroyed before the war."

"War?" Lisa asked. "What war?"

Scott looked strangely at Lisa. Then he told her what Jason had told him. When he was finished, Lisa stepped back in horror.

"That's horrible," she said. Scott looked at Lisa, surprised.

"You think so?" he asked. Lisa nodded.

"It's wrong, it's bad, and it's horrendous!"

"Ahhh!" Paul screamed clutching his head. Scott looked at Lisa puzzled.

"He's allergic to big words," Lisa explained.

"You really think what LOEP is doing is wrong?' Scott asked. Lisa then realized what she had just said.

"Of course not," she said curtly. It, .. it's a good plan. It's evil." Lisa then walked out of Scott's room. Peter and Paul followed her. Just before Peter left the room, he turned around.

"The…. Bye the way, we're guarding your room so don't try any funky business."

Lisa glared at Peter.

"Peter!" she said angrily."Did I say you could talk to him?"

"No. Sorry, boss."

"Close the door."

"Okay, boss." Scott watched as the door closed.

Meanwhile, Michael hung up the phone.

"Who did you call?" Nina asked.

"John," Michael replied. "He's going to meet us in front of P.S. 244 tomorrow. John knows P.S. 244 very well. He can help us." Michael turned to James and Nina.

"I came up with a plan," he said confidently."John will lead us to the basement. Once there, I'll look for Scott. You will fend off the bullies. Once I find Scott, you two go back to the entrance. This way we'll have a safe way to travel after Scott is rescued."

"Sounds good," James commended. "We can keep in touch with the walkie-talkie." Michael nodded. An hour later, James and Nina left. Michael then went up to his room and finished his homework. After he was finished, he laid on his bed, thinking about all that had happened to him. Sleep eventually overtook him.

The next day Michael got up. He did his usual morning routine. However, Paperboy rode his Papermobile to P.S. 244 instead of P.S. 266. There he met Velocity, Tsunami and John.

"Paperboy!" John exclaimed," It's nice to see you again!"

"Is everybody ready?" Paperboy asked. Velocity, Tsunami and John nodded.

"Then let's save Scott," Paperboy said confidently. Paperboy walked to the entrance of P.S. 244.

"There will be twenty bullies at the entrance," John warned.

"Stay back, John. We'll handle this," Paperboy said, pointing to Velocity and Tsunami.

Paperboy opened the door. Instead of seeing twenty bullies, Paperboy saw the ScizzorMen. Once the ScizzorMen saw Paperboy, they took out their scissor guns. ScizzorMan C stepped back and took out a walkie-talkie.

"He's here," ScizzorMan C said. ScizzorMan A attacked Paperboy with his scissors. Paperboy dodged the attack and threw a PBB at

ScizzorMan A. Before ScizzorMan A could react to this attack, Paperboy grabbed him with his paper claw and swung him into ScizzorMan B. Both ScizzorMen fell to the floor. Velocity skated in and attacked ScizzorMan C with his protractors. ScizzorMan C also fell to the floor.

"Hurry!" Paperboy screamed. All of a sudden, ScizzorMan B fired his scissor gun at Paperboy. Before the scissor could hit Paperboy, it was deflected by a blast of water. Tsunami ran in and fired her water pen at ScizzorMan B. She followed Velocity and Paperboy as they turned a corner. John ran after her.

Meanwhile, Jason smiled. He was in the principal's office with Shorty Scarface.

"They're here," Jason uttered as he made a paper airplane.

"Do not let them free Scott," Shorty ordered.

"They won't be able to free Scott," Jason said as he colored the paper airplane black. "They will never make it."

Chapter 9

The Trio's Drawback

Acquittal

Forestation

Insufficient

Pulchritude

NINE

Paperboy, Velocity, Tsunami and John ran down a hallway and turned a corner.

"Almost there," John uttered. "This way." The three heroes followed John. John ran down two more hallways. At the end of the last hallway, he turned a corner and then stopped. At the end of the hallway was a door.

"That's the basement door," John said looking at the unguarded door. "But something's not right. There are usually bullies guarding the door."

"It might be a trap," Velocity warned.

"We'll have to take a chance," Paperboy answered. Paperboy walked to the door. Velocity, Tsunami and John followed him. "It's open," he said.

John shook his head. "It's usually locked."

Paperboy ignored this and entered. The others followed him. Inside, Paperboy found a stairway. He walked down the stairway to the basement. The others followed close behind him. Paperboy saw doors guarded by one bully each. He turned around.

"If they have set up a trap for us down there, somebody should be by the door. Just in case."

Paperboy turned to John. "John, can you go back now? We can handle things from here. Thanks for your help."

John nodded." If I see any trouble, I'll call you."

"Alright," Paperboy agreed. Paperboy waited as John went back up the stairway. He turned to Velocity and Tsunami.

"How do we find Scott?" Paperboy asked.

"I've been thinking about that," Velocity answered. "But I don't have an answer yet."

Paperboy thought for a minute. He had an idea. "I'll shout,"

"Shout?" Tsunami asked.

"Yeah," Paperboy answered. "I'll shout for Scott. You two will have to handle the bullies. Trust me, I rescued John the same way."

"Okay," Tsunami said flatly. "But don't take a long time to find him."
Paperboy nodded. He stepped out in clear view of the bullies.

One of the bullies spotted him and shouted, "He's here! He's here!"

The trio heard the bully's shout. Lisa took out a walkie-talkie.

"Lisa to Jason," she said. "Paperboy's here. Hurry."

"Who's here, boss?" Paul asked.

"The enemy," Lisa said confidently.

"Oh," Paul uttered. " Well, they're wrong then."

"What?" Lisa asked turning to Paul. But she was too late.

"Everybody!" Paul shouted. "Scott's not over there, he's in here!"

"Paul!" Lisa roared, "Be quiet."

Paperboy overhead Paul's shout. He looked at the door the trio was guarding.

"Scott," he whispered, "I'm coming." Paperboy started to run to the trio.

"Get him," a bully ordered. Paperboy ran faster to Scott's room. Suddenly, a bully knocked Paperboy to the floor. The bully got up, picked up Paperboy and was about to punch him. But before he could, he was splashed with water. The bully fell to the floor, drenched. Paperboy turned around. He saw Tsunami and Velocity.

"Keep moving," Tsunami ordered. Paperboy turned around and continued to run to Scott's room. Another bully approached Paperboy from behind. Paperboy spotted him as he leaped towards him. Paperboy turned around and grabbed the bully's hand with his paper claw. He swung the bully away from him. Paperboy continued running in the direction of Scott's room. He finally made it to Scott's door. And to the trio!

"So, we meet again, Paperboy," Lisa remarked. "Unfortunately, this will be the last time we will ever meet."

"Scott!" Paperboy shouted. "Scott! Are you okay?" Scott heard the shouts and ran to the door.

"Mic….I mean, Paperboy!" Scott shouted from the other side of the room. Paperboy sighed in relief. His brother was okay.

"I'm coming Scott," Paperboy shouted, "You'll be free soon!"

Lisa chuckled. "That's not going to happen." She turned to Paul and Peter. "Attack him," she ordered. Without hesitation, Paul and Peter walked to Paperboy.

"Three people are guarding my door," Scott shouted from inside.

"I can see that," Paperboy answered. "But which one has the key?"

Lisa smiled and took a key out her pocket. She held it up so Paperboy could clearly see.

"Come and get it," she taunted.

Paperboy started to run for the key. Suddenly, Paul grabbed Paperboy. Paperboy instinctively used his paper claw. The attack barely hurt Paul. Paul tightened his grip.

"This is not good," Paperboy whispered. Paul then punched him. Paperboy fell several feet back, hit the wall then fell to the floor. Peter ran towards Paperboy. Before Peter reached him Paperboy got up and fired a PBB at Peter. The PBB hit Peter but barely hurt him. Peter stopped and stared angrily at his paper cut. He then rushed to Paperboy. Once close enough, he kicked Paperboy. Paperboy flew to the wall. He hit the wall very hard then slowly sank to the floor.

"Ohhh," he groaned.

Peter then picked Paperboy up and swung him to the other wall. Paperboy hit the wall, bounced off and collapsed on the floor.

"Paperboy, are you alright?" Scott shouted. There was no reply.

"Paperboy! Paperboy," Scott shouted.

Lisa turned to Paul. "Destroy him," she ordered. Without questioning, Paul and Peter walked to Paperboy.

Meanwhile, Jason and the ScizzorMen raced to the basement door. Jason had contacted the ScizzorMen after Lisa told him Paperboy was in the bascment. Now they were all running to the basement door to complete their plan. Jason and the ScizzorMen dashed down two hallways and turned the corner. They saw John in front of the basement door. John looked at Jason and the ScizzorMen in horror. He turned towards the door.

"Help!" he shouted. "Somebody, help me!"

Nearby, Velocity stopped a bully. He heard John's cry.

"John," Velocity cried. Velocity looked around. Tsunami was fighting another bully. And Paperboy was trying to save Scott.

"It's up to me," Velocity thought. Hc raced to the stairway.

"Help," John screamed as Jason and the ScizzorMen walked up to him. ScizzorMan A grabbed John and covered his mouth.

"I'll take him," Jason said. "Go down there and overwhelm them."

The ScizzorMen nodded. ScizzorMan A handed John to Jason.

"We'll tell you when the job is finished." Jason nodded. The ScizzorMen opened the door and stepped inside. Before they could close it, Velocity raced up the stairway. Before the ScizzorMen could react to his presence, Velocity pushed through them and exited the door. He closed the door behind him. ScizzorMan B angrily walked to the door.

"No," ScizzorMan C announced. "We have to stick to the plan. We have to overwhelm Paperboy and his friends. Somebody else will catch him. Let's go."

ScizzorMan B walked away from the door.

Velocity stood up and saw Jason and John. Thinking quickly, Jason threw John to Velocity. He then ran to the door, took out a key and locked it. Velocity saw this. He pushed John aside and said, "What are you doing?"

Jason smiled. "I just sealed Paperboy's fate. It's only a matter of time now." Velocity skated to Jason.

"Give me that key!" he bellowed. Jason put the key in his pocket and grabbed Velocity.

"AHHH," Velocity cried out in pain. Jason swung Velocity away from him. He then grabbed John.

"No!", John cried.

"You're coming with me." Jason carried John away.

Velocity stood up. He looked at the paper cut that remained where Jason had grabbed him.

"A paper claw?" Velocity said in bewilderment.

Meanwhile, Paperboy was having no luck defeating the trio. In desperation, he took out his paper laser and fired at Paul.

"Stop!" Paul screamed. He then grabbed Paperboy and started choking him.

"Paperboy!" Scott screamed. In his room, Scott was worried about his brother.

"How could Paperboy defeat Paul and Peter?" Suddenly Scott remembered something about Paul.

"Paperboy!" he shouted. "One of them is allergic to big words!"

Paperboy heard what Scott had said. It sounded ridiculous but it was worth a try. He thought of the words he has studied in school.

"Acquittal," Paperboy barely managed to say.

"Huh?" Paul said dropping Paperboy. Paperboy rubbed his neck.

"Acquittal!" Paperboy screamed.

"Ahhhh!" Paul wailed as he clutched his head. Paperboy cleared his throat.

"Forestation!" Paperboy screamed.

"Ahhhh!" Paul continued to wail. Paul ran to Peter and punched him with all his strength. Peter fell to the floor.

"Make it stop!" Paul begged.

"Insufficient!" Paperboy screamed.

"Ahhh!" Paul roared as he ran to Lisa. He grabbed Lisa and shook her.

"Make it stop!" he railed. Paul shook Lisa so violently that she dropped the key.

"Paul, control yourself. Stop!" Lisa pleaded. Paperboy quickly grabbed the key.

"Pulchritude!" Paperboy yelled.

"Ahhhh!" Paul roared. He dropped Lisa and covered his ears.

"I can't stand it," Paul screamed.

Paperboy quickly used the key and opened Scott's door. Scott stood in front of it.

"Scott!" Paperboy yelled in joy.

"Ahhh," Paul screamed again.

Paperboy noticed the cut on Scott's face. "What happened?" he asked.

"No time to explain," Scott said as he stepped out of the room.

Paperboy and Scott exited the room. They saw Paul on the ground, eyes open in shock.

"You took my advice," Scott said.

"Yeah," Paperboy answered. "Now let's get out of here before he recovers." Paperboy and Scott ran to Tsunami as she splashed a bully with water. Suddenly another bully grabbed her from behind. Paperboy attacked the bully with his paper airplane. The bully fell to the ground.

"Let's go," Paperboy said.

Tsunami sighed in relief. "Took you long enough. I don't know if I can take too much more of this."

All of a sudden, the ScizzorMen came down the hallway. They spotted Paperboy and smiled.

"More enemies!" Tsunami said in disbelief.

"Run!" Paperboy screamed. Paperboy, Tsunami and Scott quickly ran up the stairway and to the door. Paperboy tried to open the door but it wouldn't open.

"It's locked," Paperboy exclaimed.

"We're trapped," Tsunami uttered.

"Where is James?" Scott asked.

Tsunami tapped her walkie-talkie twice. "James?" she asked.

"Yeah," Velocity answered.

"Where are you?"

"I'm in the hallway. Jason locked the door and kidnapped John. I can't find him."

"Jason locked the door?" Tsunami said.

"Yeah. He has the key."

"James," Tsunami said in a sad and threatening way, "You better find Jason. And you better find him fast." She then heard footsteps coming up the stairway.

"We can't fight for much longer. Find Jason and get the key quickly."

"I don't have any idea where he is!" Velocity said, confused.

"Just find him, James," Tsunami said as she saw a bully come up the stairway. "If you don't, we're all doomed."

——Chapter 10——
Velocity's Worst Nightmare

TEN

Velocity skated down a hallway.

"John!" he called. There was no answer. "John," he called again. Velocity hopelessly skated down another hallway. "I have to find him before it's too late.".

Meanwhile, Jason carried John up a different stairway. At the end of the stairway was a door.

"Help!" John screamed. Jason opened the door and threw John through the door. John landed on the pavement hard. He got up and gasped. John looked up at the sky. He looked around him. He was on a moderately sized platform. Nothing else was on the platform.

"Welcome to the roof," Jason said in an evil tone. "Take in everything that you see." Jason grabbed John and dragged him to the edge of the roof. He forced John's head down.

"Oh no," John said as he looked at the ground below. It was about forty feet below. Jason pushed John further away from the edge. John stepped back in horror as Jason approached him.

"Ready to drop?" Jason asked. John stumbled and fell on the pavement. Jason ran to him and grabbed him.

"No!" John screamed as Jason carried him to the edge of the roof once more. "Somebody help me!"

Jason held John by his shirt as he carried him further towards the edge of the roof. John was now struggling to save himself. Jason held him up in the air and smiled. Once he let go of John's shirt, John would fall to the ground. His smile grew wider as he recalled that the ground was forty feet below. He looked down at a struggling John.

"You better stop struggling," Jason said smiling. " I might lose my grip."

John was horrified. "Somebody help me!" he screamed at the top of his lungs.

"I've had enough of your pitiful screams," Jason said angrily. He smiled again. "Goodbye," he said wickedly.

Jason was about to drop John when he heard a faint voice coming from inside P.S. 244. Jason remembered Velocity.

"He's not very far away," Jason uttered. Jason then looked at John. He then came up with an evil plan. He pulled John up and away from the edge. He swung him away from him, close to the stairway. John hit the pavement hard. Jason walked up to him and smiled.

"Wha…. What are you going to do with me?" John asked terrified. Jason's smile grew wider as he stood over John.

"You're not completely useless," he said in John's voice.

Meanwhile, the bullies had just reached the stairway to the basement.

Tsunami looked at Paperboy. "We have to keep fighting," she said. Paperboy nodded his head.

"I don't know how much longer I can keep fighting. I just hope it will be enough time for James to get us out of here."

All of a sudden a bully ran to Tsunami and punched her. Caught off guard, she fell to the floor. Paperboy attacked the bully with his paper airplane. He swung the bully away from him and Tsunami.

"I'm not going to watch this," Scott said. He walked to Paperboy.

"Give me a paper airplane." Paperboy handed Scott one of his two paper airplanes. Scott put the paper airplane between his pointer and middle finger. Tsunami stood up.

"We must get out of here if we are to survive," she said.

"Then let's go," Paperboy replied. Paperboy, Tsunami and Scott ran to the stairway. There they saw four bullies coming up the stairs. These were followed by another large group of bullies. Paperboy ran to one bully and attacked him with his paper airplane. The bully fell to the ground. Tsunami blasted another bully with water and that bully also fell to the ground. Scott grabbed another bully and swung him into another bully. Both fell to the floor. Scott then picked up one of the bullies and threw him to one of the bullies that were coming up the stairway. The bully fell down. Scott then pushed the three remaining bullies into the other bullies.

"That will slow them down," Scott said

"But it won't stop them," Tsunami answered.

Half a minute later, a bully started to come up the stairway. Other bullies followed him.

"What do we do now?" Tsunami asked. Paperboy took out two paper lasers. He handed one to Scott and then aimed at the bully.

"We're going to stop them," he replied. Paperboy fired his paper laser. The paper balls hit the bully and he stepped back. He then began to move forward one step at a time.

"I need help!" Paperboy shouted. Tsunami and Scott nodded. Tsunami fired her water pen at the bully and Scott fired his paper laser. The bully then retreated down the stairway. The bully behind him was hit by the water and paper laser. He also retreated down the stairway. The other bully behind the second one did the same thing. One by one, all the other bullies followed.

"Bullies are not very smart and they all think alike", Paperboy remembered.

"It's working!" Tsunami said happily as she blasted another bully with water.

"Retreat!" the bully shouted. He then ran down the stairway. Paperboy looked just to make sure. No more bullies were coming up the stairway. Paperboy sighed in relief. One minute passed then

Paperboy spotted someone coming up the stairway. Paperboy gasped. It was Peter! Tsunami and Scott also saw Peter. They all fired their weapons. Paperboy fired his paper laser. Peter ignored the attack and just continued his way up the stairway.

"Oh no," Paperboy whispered.

Meanwhile, Velocity desperately searched for John.

"John!" he screamed.

"I'm here," a voice replied. Velocity smiled. He skated in the direction of the voice. Velocity found himself at the bottom of a stairway. John was in front of a closed door. John raced down the stairway to Velocity.

"I'm glad you're here!" John said as he reached the bottom of the stairway.

"It's good to see you," Velocity said quickly. "But where's Copycat?"

"Up there," John pointed. "I barely escaped from him. Any minute now he's going to open the door and come after me. Don't let him get me."

"Wait here," Velocity ordered. "Copycat has the key to the basement. Without it, I can't free Paperboy and Tsunami. I'm going to get that key." Velocity ignored the knapsack on the bottom of the stairway and ran up the stairs.

"Okay," John said smiling. "I'll wait here."

Velocity reached the top of the stairway. He walked to the door and opened it. He skated through the door. He stopped once he saw where he was.

"I'm on the roof," Velocity realized as he looked up at the sky. Velocity looked around. He spotted someone in a protractor trap. Velocity looked more closely. He gasped. It was John! Velocity cut the ropes with his protractors. Once John was free he said, "It's a trap! Copycat's down there!"

"What?" Velocity asked in surprise.

"I'm the real John! Copycat is dressed up like me!" John took the protractor out of his foot and stood up.

"We now have to get out of here!" he screamed. Velocity reached for the door. But before he could open it, the door opened. Nightmare stood at the door.

"You're not Nightmare, you're Copycat," Velocity declared. Copycat chuckled.

"I guess I can't fool you this time."

"Give me the key," Velocity ordered.

"Do you know why I got you up here?" Copycat asked Velocity. Velocity did not answer.

"I thought it would be more entertaining if you watched him here,"

Copycat said, pointing to John. "Or vice-versa. It doesn't matter to me. Because either way, you will both fall off the roof." Suddenly, Copycat attacked Velocity with his terror airplane. Velocity fell. He quickly got up and counter attacked with his protractors. Copycat dodged the attack and threw a TBB at Velocity. Velocity cried out in pain. Copycat tripped Velocity then picked him up. Velocity managed to attack again with his protractors. Before Copycat could react, Velocity kicked him to the ground. Copycat quickly got up. He took out a terror laser and fired at Velocity. Velocity deflected the black paper balls with his protractor. Copycat threw another terror laser at Velocity. Velocity stepped back in surprise. Copycat sensed this and punched Velocity who fell right at the edge of the roof. Velocity slowly got up. Copycat threw another TBB. Velocity stepped back a little.

"Oh," he managed to say as he tried to balance himself on the edge of the roof. Copycat smiled. He then threw one of his terror airplanes.

"No!" John screamed. John ran to Copycat. Copycat turned around and kicked John. John hit the floor right outside the door. Copycat turned around in time to see the terror airplane hit Velocity. Velocity fell back … and slid towards the edge of the roof of P.S. 244. He instinctively shot out his hand and grabbed the edge of the roof. He managed to lift the other hand up to the edge of the roof. Velocity looked up in horror at Copycat, who was standing on the edge of the roof, waiting to destroy him.

Meanwhile, Peter was almost up the stairway. Paperboy, Scott and Tsunami continued to fire their weapons. These weapons had no effect on Peter and he continued up the stairway. He finally reached the top. He then punched Paperboy. Paperboy hit the wall and fell to the floor. Scott looked at Peter.

"Deposition!" he yelled. Peter kicked Tsunami and then faced Scott.

"Oh No," Scott uttered, " Wrong one." Peter then punched Scott. Scott flew to the wall and then landed on the floor. All of a sudden, Paul appeared in the stairway. Peter grabbed Tsunami and threw her to Paul. Paul caught her and threw her in the basement. Peter then threw Scott to Paul. Paul caught him and threw him in the basement also.

Paperboy quickly got up. But before he could do anything, Peter grabbed him and threw him to Paul who caught him and in turn threw him into the basement. Paperboy landed on the floor hard. He saw Tsunami and Scott lying beside him. What Paperboy saw next scared him. The ScizzorMen and all the other bullies were all around him but formed an incomplete circle. Peter and Paul came down and filled in the missing space. Paperboy stood up. Tsunami and

Scott also stood up. The circle of bullies then started to close in on

Paperboy. Paperboy tapped his walkie-talkie.

"James!" Paperboy yelled. "Hurry! I'm running out of time."

From the roof Velocity had heard what Paperboy said. "I'm running out of time too," He thought frantically for a moment and then reality set in. He remembered the situation he was in. Copycat stood on the edge of the roof while he was hanging on to the edge for his life. Copycat smiled. He stepped on Velocity's hand. Velocity continued to hang on. But he could slowly feel his fingers slipping from the pain…

"This is how it ends," Copycat declared. "You die from a fatal fall while Paperboy and your other friends die from the attacks of our army of bullies."

Velocity remembered what Paperboy had said through the walkie-talkie. All of a sudden, one of Velocity hands slipped. He looked at his hand. He then had an idea. He threw the protractor at Copycat with the hand that slipped while holding on with the other hand.

"Ahhhh," Copycat cried out in pain. Copycat stepped back and off of Velocity's hand. Velocity then pulled himself up from the edge of the roof. He stood up and attacked Copycat fiercely with his protractors. Before Copycat could react, Velocity kicked him. Copycat flew to the door. He got up angrily. Velocity skated to Copycat and tripped him. Copycat fell to the floor again. He then took out a paper laser. Velocity quickly grabbed Copycat and swung him away from him. Copycat landed on the edge of the roof.

"No," he whispered, "It won't end like this." He quickly threw a TBB at Velocity. Velocity cried out in pain. Copycat got up and raced to Velocity. He grabbed him with the black paper claw. But before Copycat could do anything else, Velocity kicked him hard. Copycat stumbled back. Velocity then punched Copycat with all his strength. Copycat fell back and slipped towards the edge of the roof but reacted quickly and clung to the edge. He looked up in horror to see Velocity standing at the edge of the roof.

"No," Copycat begged, "Don't make me fall. I'll give you the key. Just don't make me fall. I'm scared of heights, you know. I don't want to die. Please….please," he pleaded sincerely.

"Give me the key now!" Velocity ordered. Copycat reached in this pocket with one hand and pulled out the key. He then threw it on the roof. Velocity quickly picked up the key. He returned to the edge of the roof and looked at Copycat. Copycat started begging and pleading again.

"Don't make me fall," Copycat pleaded. "I'll do anything, anything you want."

"Anything?" Velocity asked.

"Anything!" Copycat answered.

"Well, guess what, Jason?' Velocity uttered. "From this moment you're not a part of LOEP anymore. You will renounce membership in that organization. Do you understand?"

"Okay!" Copycat screamed. "I'm not part of LOEP anymore. Now please help me! I'm slipping and I'm scared."

Velocity quickly set up a protractor trap. He then pulled Copycat up and into the trap.

"If I were you, I wouldn't roll around too much. You might get close to the edge again," Velocity said. He then exited the door. John was outside the door.

"You're okay!" he exclaimed.

"Let's go!" Velocity replied. Copycat watched as Velocity and John left. It was then he realized what he had just done to himself.

Velocity skated to the basement with John running close behind him. In less than a minute, Velocity reached the door. He used the key from Copycat and opened the door. He and John raced down the stairway. He looked in horror as he saw many, many bullies attacking Paperboy, Tsunami and Scott.

"Hey!" Velocity yelled. Some of the bullies turned around to face Velocity.

"Another enemy," a bully shouted.

"Who wants to obliterate me?" Velocity shouted.

"Exterminate," Paperboy shouted.

"Ahhh!" Paul screamed. Paul attacked several bullies. "Make it stop," he screamed. He punched ScizzorMan A. The bullies tried desperately to control Paul but to no avail. He began attacking all the bullies. Tsunami and Scott saw this and quickly ran to Velocity and John. They all ran up the stairway, out the door, out the hallways, and out of P.S. 244. Once outside, Paperboy sighed in relief. He walked home with his friends.

Scott sighed once he was at Michael's house. He made a silent vow to himself never to work alone. Not when he had friends willing to help him.

At PS 266, Mr. Raptor sat in a chair in total defeat. He had tried everything but he just could not capture Paperboy. "If only the principal understood what Paperboy was doing," Mr. Raptor said to himself. Suddenly, Mr. Raptor had an idea.

"The principal," he repeated. "Only the principal can stop Paperboy."

Mr. Raptor smiled.

"There is going to be a new principal at P.S. 266."

Later that day, the trio and the ScizzorMen entered the principal's office. In the office, Shorty Scarface was looking out the window. He turned to face the trio and the ScizzorMen.

"Well?" he asked. ScizzorMan B lowered his head.

"They escaped the trap." ScizzorMen B said sadly.

"What!" Shorty yelled. He sighed. "Could this get any worse?"

"Um…. I saw Copycat while on the way here," Lisa uttered. "He said he was defeated in battle. He's no longer a member of LOEP."

Shorty looked at Lisa in disbelief and anger.

"I'm tired of Paperboy, Scott, James and Nina foiling my plans," Shorty said angrily. "Now, Copycat's gone. Just like ScizzorMan. If this continues, LOEP will fall!" Shorty stared angrily at the other ScizzorMen and Lisa. Suddenly, Copycat's idea came back to Shorty. He sighed.

"It's the only way,' he whispered. "It's the only way to destroy my enemies and take over P.S. 266." Shorty looked at the ScizzorMen and Lisa.

"I'm putting you two in charge of preparations. ScizzorMan A, go downtown and spread the word. Lisa, Peter and Paul spread the word here at P.S. 244. LOEP is preparing for war."

Lisa's eyes widened. The ScizzorMen smiled. Shorty looked at them for a moment.

"Go!" he shouted. The trio and the ScizzorMen then exited the principal's office to carry out Shorty's orders.

Michael, Scott, James, John and Nina rested and talked about their adventures. Scott told them about his scar. He also told them about LOEP's planned war. He promised to seek revenge on LOEP by working together. James told them about his battle with Copycat on the roof. Michael and Nina told them about their battle with the ScizzorMen, Peter and Paul.

Unfortunately, little did Michael and his friends know that the worst was yet to come.

Omari Jeremiah

Omari Jeremiah is a 16 year old African American who was born in the Bronx, New York. He attended Elementary School at CES 109 and Middle School at MS 145 both in the Bronx. In Middle School he was a member of the Fieldston Enrichment Program (FEP). This is a program for academically gifted students at the Fieldston School in Riverdale, New York. Omari is presently attending the Hackley School in Tarrytown, New York and is in the 11th grade.

Omari has been writing from a very early age. He has written many short stories and poems in elementary, middle and high school. His first published book, Paperboy, was written when he was only 12 years old and in the 7th grade at Middle School 145. He wrote Paperboy II: Overwhelming Odds when he was 13 years old. This was followed by Paperboy III: The School of Doom when he was 14 years old.

The Paperboy Series consists of six books. Omari completed the remaining three books in the series at age 14. His fourth book Paperboy IV: L.O.E.P.'S Worst Nightmare clearly demonstrates the imagination, creativity, humor, and story telling ability of this young and talented author.

Omari is an avid reader and his other interests include football, tennis, ping-pong and weight-lifting. He wants to be a professional author and publisher.

He presently resides in the Bronx with his parents, an older sister and an older brother.